To my really BIG sons, Dylan, Connor,
and Chris Paratore.
I'm so proud of you and love you so much.
~ C.P.

For Scottie, Elle, and Hope,
who inspire me to be BIG.
~ C.F.

Library of Congress Cataloging-in-Publication Data is available.
Library of Congress Catalog Card Number 2012942574

ISBN 978-0-9829938-5-9

16 15 14 13 12   1 2 3 4 5 6 7 8 9 10

Printed in Canada
First edition 2012

Little Pickle Press LLC
PO Box 983, Belvedere, CA 94920

Please visit us at www.littlepicklepress.com.

Be the biggest YOU that you can be!
Coleen 2013

BIG

Written by **COLEEN PARATORE**

Illustrated by **CLARE FENNELL**

Little Pickle Press

When you were little,
You wanted to be **BIG**.

Big enough to . . .
reach that, **ride** this,
play here, **go** there.

How about now? Are you **BIG** yet?

When, **exactly**, does **BIG** happen?

Some people say **BIG** is measured by **years**, or **weight**, or **inches**.

Others think **BIG** is how **rich** you are or where you live or how much **stuff** you own.

Those people are **wrong**.

BIG is **bigger** than that. **BIG** is **more**.

BIG

is being

bright.

BIG is being **healthy**.

BIG

is being

imaginative.

BIG is being the **biggest** YOU that YOU can be.

BIG is being **kind**.

BIG is being **helpful**.

BIG is being a **valuable** member of your family, school, and neighborhood.

BIG is being the **biggest** **YOU** that **YOU** can be.

BIG

is being an

active

citizen

of your

city, country,

world.

BIG is being a friend to the Earth.
BIG is being a friend to yourself.

BIG is being the **biggest** YOU that YOU can be.

Each and **every** year, every person

on the planet gets 365 presents. You . . . me . . .

everybody.

September 4th

October 10th

Brand new day

Brand new day

6th July

OCTOBER 19TH

365 brand NEW days.

And **every** day,
in countless ways,
we can choose
to be little—
or we can choose
to be **BIG**.

20TH JANUARY

Brand new day

But **how** will you know **when** you have **succeeded**?
How will you know **when** you're **BIG**?

How can I be **BIG** healthy today?

How can I be **BIG** in my family today?

How can I be a **BIG** friend to the planet today?

I'm proud of myself. I'm **BIG**!

How can I be a **BIG** friend to myself today?

I learned from my mistake today. I'm **BIG**!

How can I be **BIG** in my community today?

How can I be **BIG** kind today?

That was a good choice. I'm **BIG**!

You won't get a trophy,

a diploma, or an award.

The **reward** for being
BIG is **invisible**.

It's a pride **inside**,
a **feeling** of **goodness**
that makes its home
in **your heart**.

And here's an

IMPORTANT

thing to remember.

BIG doesn't

happen

all at once.

BIG happens **little** by **little** . . .

one **little** thought,

one **little** question,

one **little** action,

one **little** change,

one **little** way,

one little **day at a time**.

And **all** together, **all** of those "**ones**" add up to one **wonderful**, very big, **YOU**.

How many little **ways** can **you** think of to be . . .

Our Mission

Little Pickle Press is dedicated to helping parents and educators cultivate conscious, responsible little people by stimulating explorations of the meaningful topics of their generation through a variety of media, technologies, and techniques.

Little Pickle Press
Environmental Benefits Statement

This book is printed on Appleton Utopia U2:XG Extra Green Paper. It is made with 30% PCRF (Post-Consumer Recovered Fiber) and Green Power. It is FSC®-certified, acid-free, and ECF (Elemental Chlorine-Free). All of the electricity required to manufacture the paper used to print this book is matched with RECS (Renewable Energy Credits) from Green-e® certified energy sources, primarily wind.

Little Pickle Press saved the following resources by using U2:XG paper:

trees	energy	greenhouse gases	wastewater	solid waste
Post-consumer recovered fiber displaces wood fiber with savings translated as trees.	PCRF content displaces energy used to process equivalent virgin fiber.	Measured in CO_2 equivalents, PCRF content and Green Power reduce greenhouse gas emissions.	PCRF content eliminates wastewater needed to process equivalent virgin fiber.	PCRF content eliminates solid waste generated by producing an equivalent amount of virgin fiber through the pulp and paper manufacturing process.
71 trees	**41.5 mil BTUs**	**11,348 lbs**	**30,188 gal**	**3,844 lbs**

Calculations based on research by Environmental Defense Fund and other members of the Paper Task Force.

 B Corporations are a new type of company that uses the power of business to solve social and environmental problems. Little Pickle Press is proud to be a Certified B Corporation.

About the **Author**

Having published seventeen books in her first eight years as an author, Coleen Murtagh Paratore shares what she has learned about writing for young people with great enthusiasm. Every time she speaks about writing, she holds up her library card and says, "I am a writer because I was a reader." She credits her mother with taking her on the bus to the city library each Saturday to collect her "treasures" for the week.

Coleen now lives in Troy, NY, and is the proud mother of three BIG sons, Christopher, Connor, and Dylan. In addition to writing, she gives presentations at state and national conferences and book festivals, as well as visiting schools across the country, where she enjoys meeting librarians, teachers, parents, and students.

Visit her at www.coleenparatore.com.

About the **Illustrator**

Having left university with an illustration degree and after fifteen years as a designer and studio manager in the UK greeting card industry, Clare, a mum to Ella (age ten) and Hope (seven), took the plunge and decided to follow her life-long dream to illustrate children's books.

So having quit her job, Clare ousted her hubby from his beloved study, set deep in the English countryside, and promptly converted it to a rather messy studio filled with children's picture books, cats, cushions, pencils, and paint. Clare set to work carving out her new career as a children's book illustrator!

Some two short years later, Clare is joyfully collaging the contents of her imagination into the pages of children's books and loving every moment.